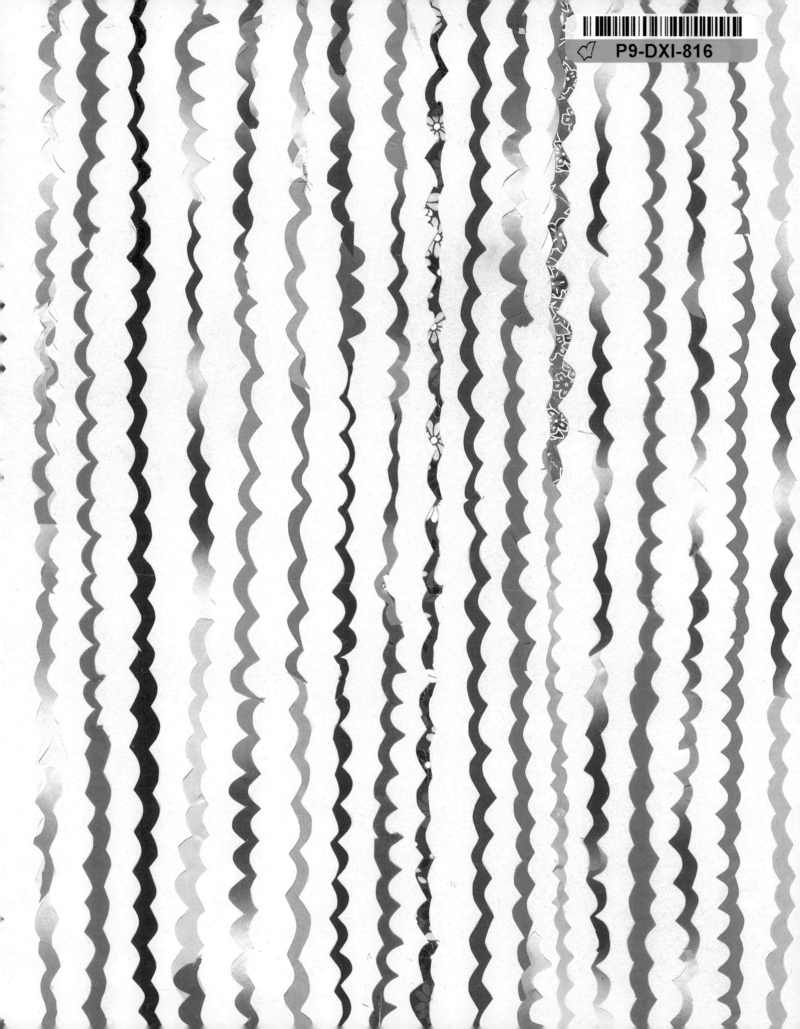

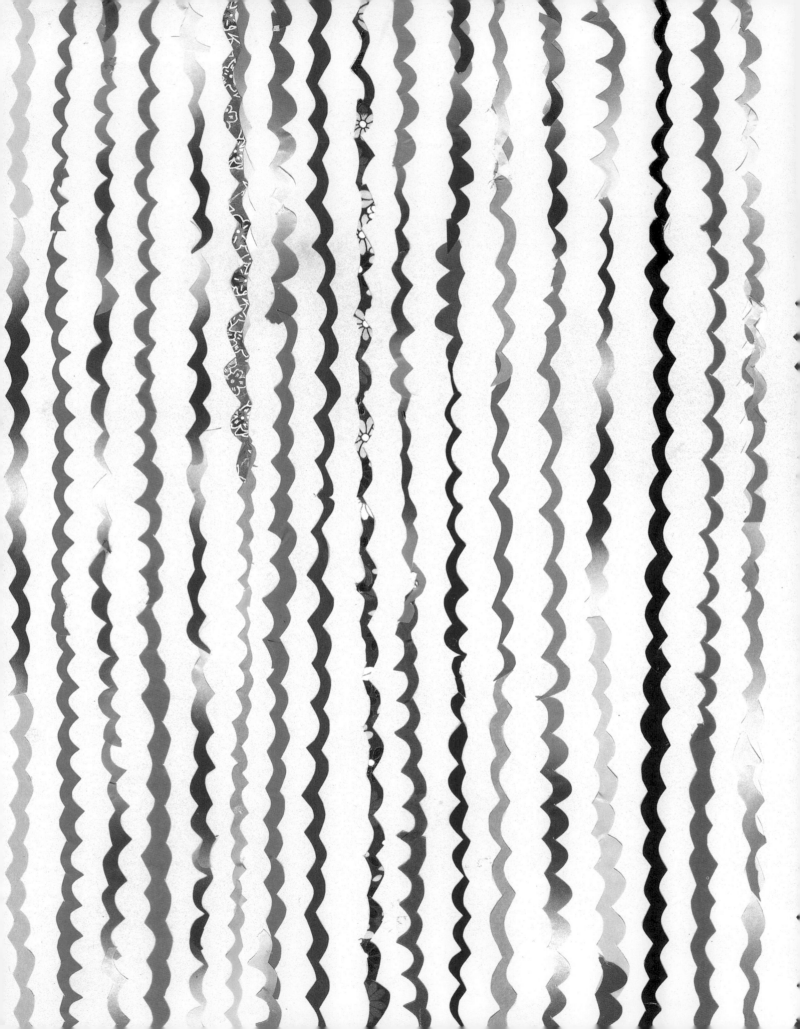

HOORAY, A PIÑATA!

Elisa Kleven

Dutton Children's Books · New York

Library of Congress Cataloging-in-Publication Data

Kleven, Elisa.
Hooray! A piñata! / by Elisa Kleven [author and illustrator].
1st ed.   p. cm.
Summary: After she chooses a cute dog piñata for her birthday
party, Clara pretends it is her pet and she doesn't want
it to get broken.
ISBN 0-525-45605-8 (hc)
[1. Piñatas—Fiction.   2. Dogs—Fiction.   3. Parties—Fiction.
4. Hispanic Americans—Fiction.]   I. Title.
PZ7.K6783875Ho   1996
[E]—dc20   95-45750   CIP   AC

Published in the United States 1996 by
Dutton Children's Books,
a division of Penguin Books USA Inc.
375 Hudson Street, New York, New York 10014
Designed by Sara Reynolds
Printed in Hong Kong
First Edition
1 3 5 7 9 10 8 6 4 2

For Mia, who loves piñatas

With special thanks to Paul,
Sean, Donna, and Sara

Clara's birthday was coming. "I'm going to have a cake at my party," she told her friend Samson.

"Of course you'll have a cake," said Samson. "There's always cake at birthday parties."

"And I'm going to have balloons," Clara said.

"Everyone has balloons," said Samson.

"And I'm going to have a piñata, too," Clara added proudly. "Mama's taking me to pick one out this morning. Want to come?"

"Hooray, a piñata!" Samson clapped his hands. "I love piñatas!"

"I love piñatas, too," said Clara as her mother led them to the
piñata store. "I love to fill them with candy."

"I love to whack them," Samson said.

"And smack them and crack them," said Clara.

"And mash and smash and break them!" cried Samson.

"And watch the candy fall!" yelled Clara.

"And eat the candy!" shouted Samson.

There were so many piñatas to choose from. Donkeys and dinosaurs, peacocks and stars, robots and ice-cream cones, lions and lambs, all ruffly and fluffy in their bright paper curls.

There were even some monster piñatas. Samson made a face at

a big, jagged one. "Get this scary thundercloud monster, Clara!"

"A thundercloud monster?" Clara shook her head. "I like this little dog. Can I get him, Mama?"

"If that's the one you want," said her mother.

"He's the one," said Clara.

"That dog is so small, he won't hold very much candy," Samson told her.

"I like him, though," Clara replied.

"He's a good little dog," the piñata vendor said as he lifted the piñata down. Clara took the dog in her arms. He was light and soft, and he smelled like newspaper.

Clara petted the dog's curly fur as she carried him home. "I think I'll name him Lucky."

"He looks like a Lucky," said Samson.

"He's a good little dog. We could take him to the park for a picnic."

"Mom wants me home for lunch," replied Samson. "And you should save that piñata for your birthday party. You don't want it to get wrecked."

"It won't get wrecked, don't worry," Clara assured him.

At home, Clara gave Lucky a bowl of crunchy brown cereal because it looked a little bit like dog food. Lucky seemed to enjoy it. When he had eaten, Clara made him a collar and a leash and took him out for a walk.

Along the way, they stopped
to greet people

and other dogs

and to smell bushes,
flowers, and trees.

Then they came home and dug a deep hole in the sand.

"What are you doing to that poor piñata?" Samson called from across the fence.

"Lucky's digging," Clara told him.

"He's getting all dirty," Samson replied.

"He'll shake himself clean."

"Clara, honey," called her mother. "Shake yourself clean and get your sweater. We're going to Grandma's for dinner."

"See you, Clara," Samson said. "Take care of that piñata."

"I will," Clara promised.

She held Lucky tight as the car sped across the city. Lucky sniffed the air with its many smells—salty, oily, bready, sweet. His ears flapped in the wind.

Grandma was waiting for them on her porch.

"Look, I got a dog!" Clara ran to show her.

"What a good little dog." Grandma patted him. "So quiet and so clean."

"I have to keep him clean because he's really a piñata," said Clara. "If I bathed him, his fur would fall apart."

"But you can brush him," Grandma said as they went into the house. "And you can keep him warm." She gave Clara a small crocheted blanket. "And here's a little spending money, just for you."

"Thanks, Grandma." Clara hugged her.

She knew what she would spend the money on—dog biscuits and a ride on the merry-go-round near Grandma's house.

After dinner they walked there together. As her horse galloped around and around, Clara pretended that she and Lucky were flying.

They flew in Clara's dreams that night . . .

and on her swing the
next morning.

They ate cheese
sandwiches together

and listened to stories

and bicycled around the block with Samson.

"Careful with that piñata!" Samson yelled as they raced down-hill.

"Don't worry, Samson, he's safe!"

That afternoon, Clara and Samson made paper hats for everyone who was coming to her party the next day. Clara made a little hat for Lucky.

"You like that piñata so much," Samson said. "It's going to be sad when we stuff him with candy and break him."

Clara's eyes filled with tears. "I don't want anyone to break him," she said.

"You mean you won't have a piñata at your party?" asked Samson. "No candy?"

"We can have candy in bowls," Clara suggested, though she knew it didn't sound like much fun.

Samson sighed. "You should have a real dog, Clara. Maybe I could get you a puppy for your birthday."

"I can't have a real dog," Clara said. "Dogs and cats make my mother sneeze."

"They do? That's too bad. I'll have to get you something else, then," Samson said.

"What?" asked Clara.

"I'm not sure yet. I'll think of something good."

Early the next morning, Samson came by with two presents. Clara opened the smaller one first. Inside was a rawhide bone. "For Lucky! Thanks, Samson!"

"Open the big one," Samson said.

Clara tore off the wrapping paper and saw something big and jagged and scary.

"Hooray, a piñata!" Clara clapped her hands.

"Hooray, a piñata!" Samson clapped, too.

"What a piñata!" said Clara's mother.

Clara hugged the thundercloud. "Let's fill it with candy right now."

"Before you make friends with it, too!" Samson laughed.

Clara's father helped them cut a hole in the piñata and fill it with almond bars and cinnamon swirls, strawberry rolls and taffy, tiny bags of jelly beans and shiny chocolate kisses. Then they taped the hole shut and hung the heavy thundercloud in Clara's tree.

The piñata scowled as the guests arrived at the party. It glared as they sang and ate cake.

It grinned its toothy monster grin as the children took turns trying to break it. They whacked it and cracked it and mashed it and bashed it, but still that storm cloud did not open until . . .

Clara gave it a thundering T H W A C K . . . and candy showered
down. The children whooped and hollered.

"HOORAY! HOORAY! HOORAY!" they screamed,
and ran to grab as much as they could hold.

And when they'd eaten all they could, they played with the piñata. Samson wore the scowly face as a mask. Clara turned the bottom into a hat. And Lucky chased a quick yellow lightning bolt through the grass.

A Note About Piñatas

Piñatas are gaily decorated containers filled with sweets and sometimes small toys. Piñatas are made to be broken—smashed with a stick by eager participants at birthday parties, Christmas fiestas, and other celebrations. Breaking the piñata is a challenge—the piñata is raised and lowered on a rope, while the person trying to hit it is usually blindfolded. When at last the piñata breaks, the goodies spill out, and everyone rushes to grab them.

The custom of piñata parties began about five hundred years ago in Italy, where hosts would fill fragile, pineapple-shaped pots (called *pignatte*) with small treats for their guests. Piñatas soon became popular in Spain, then traveled with the early settlers to Mexico.

In Mexico, piñata makers began constructing fanciful animal, bird, and star formations of paper around simple clay pots and decorating these creations with paint, feathers, and colored paper. Although traditional piñatas are still formed around clay vessels, most piñatas today are made of pâpier-maché (newspaper strips bound together with flour paste) and decorated with rows of tissue-paper scallops, streamers, and ruffles.

Although piñatas are usually associated with Latin American festivities, they are gaining popularity in other parts of the world. Whimsical, bright, ephemeral as blazing candles on birthday cakes, they add a special liveliness to all kinds of celebrations.

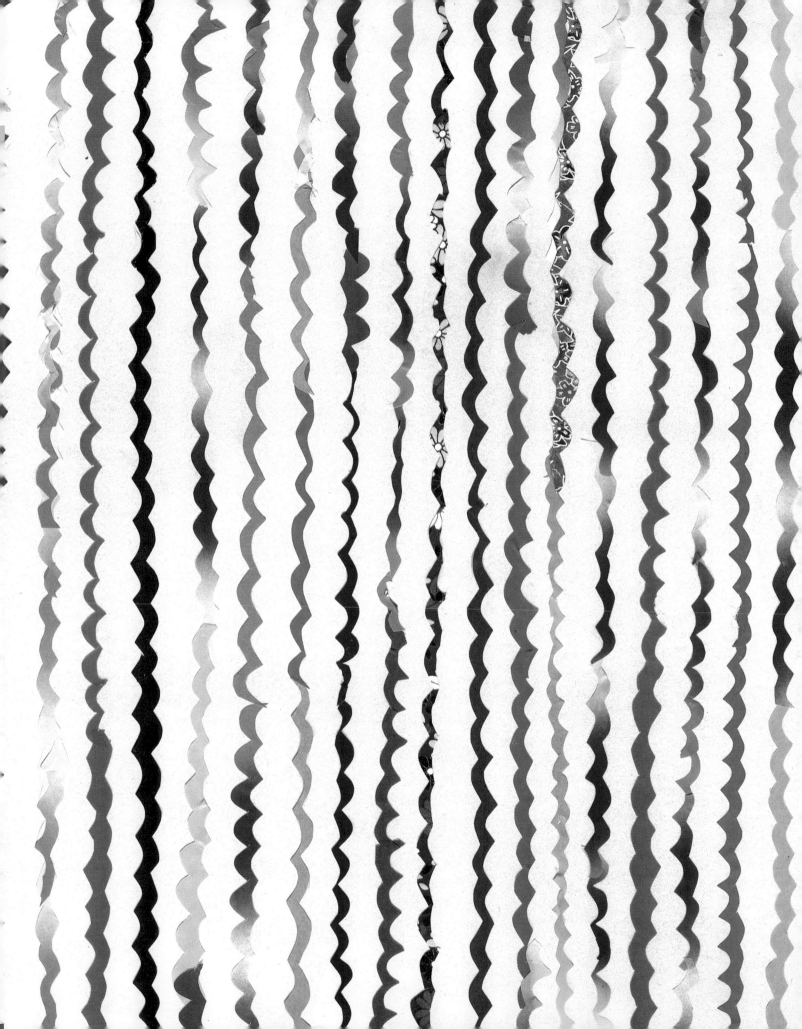